This book belongs to

_____

THE TALE OF SQUIRREL NUTKIN

BEATRIX POTTER

ILLUSTRATED BY

ALLEN ATKINSON

AN ARIEL BOOK

BANTAM BOOKS
TORONTO   NEW YORK   LONDON   SYDNEY   AUCKLAND

THE TALE OF SQUIRREL NUTKIN
A Bantam Book
April 1983

Design: Iris Bass
Editorial Director: Ron Buehl
Senior Editor: Lu Ann Walther
Production: Hal Hochvert
Art Direction: Armand Eisen

ISBN 0-553-15205-X

Bantam Books are published by Bantam Books, Inc. Its trademark,
consisting of the words "Bantam Books" and the portrayal of a rooster, is
Registered in U.S. Patent and Trademark Office and in other countries.
Marca Registrada. Bantam Books, Inc., 666 Fifth Avenue, New York,
New York 10103

Printing and binding by
Printer, industria gráfica S.A   Provenza, 388   Barcelona-25
Depósito legal B. 41012-1983
PRINTED IN SPAIN
0 9 8 7 6 5 4

The art is dedicated
to my brother,
Ronald Gunther

THIS IS A TALE about a tail—a
tail that belonged to a little red squirrel,
and his name was Nutkin.

He had a brother called Twinkleberry,
and a great many cousins:

THE TALE OF SQUIRREL NUTKIN

they lived in a
wood at the edge
of a lake.

THE TALE OF SQUIRREL NUTKIN

THE TALE OF SQUIRREL NUTKIN

In the middle of the lake there is an island covered with trees and nut bushes; and amongst those trees stands a hollow oak-tree, which is the house of an owl who is called Old Brown.

THE TALE OF SQUIRREL NUTKIN

One autumn when the nuts were ripe,
and the leaves on the hazel bushes were
golden and green—

THE TALE OF SQUIRREL NUTKIN

Nutkin and Twinkleberry and all the other little squirrels came out of the wood, and down to the edge of the lake.

THE TALE OF SQUIRREL NUTKIN

They made little rafts out of twigs, and they paddled away over the water to Owl Island to gather nuts.

THE TALE OF SQUIRREL NUTKIN

Each squirrel had a little sack and a
large oar, and spread out his tail for a sail.

They also took with them an offering of three fat mice as a present for Old Brown, and put them down upon his door-step.

Then Twinkleberry and the other little squirrels each made a low bow, and said politely—

"Old Mr. Brown, will you favour us with permission to gather nuts upon your island?"

THE TALE OF SQUIRREL NUTKIN

THE TALE OF SQUIRREL NUTKIN

But Nutkin was excessively impertinent in his manners. He bobbed up and
down like a little red *cherry*, singing—

> "Riddle me, riddle me, rot-tot-tote!
> A little wee man, in a red red coat!
> A staff in his hand, and a stone in his throat;
> If you'll tell me this riddle, I'll give you a groat."

Now this riddle is as old as the hills;
Mr. Brown paid no attention whatever to
Nutkin.

THE TALE OF SQUIRREL NUTKIN

He shut his eyes obstinately and went to sleep.

The squirrels filled their little sacks with nuts, and sailed away home in the evening.

THE TALE OF SQUIRREL NUTKIN

THE TALE OF SQUIRREL NUTKIN

THE TALE OF SQUIRREL NUTKIN

But next morning
    they all came back
        again to Owl Island;

THE TALE OF SQUIRREL NUTKIN

and Twinkleberry and the others brought a fine fat mole, and laid it on the stone in front of Old Brown's doorway, and said—

"Mr. Brown, will you favour us with your gracious permission to gather some more nuts?"

THE TALE OF SQUIRREL NUTKIN

But Nutkin, who had no respect, began to dance up and down, tickling old
Mr. Brown with a *nettle* and singing—

THE TALE OF SQUIRREL NUTKIN

"Old Mr. B! Riddle-me-ree!
Hitty Pitty within the wall,
Hitty Pitty without the wall;
If you touch Hitty Pitty,
Hitty Pitty will bite you!"

Mr. Brown woke up suddenly and carried the mole into his house.

He shut the door in Nutkin's face. Presently a little thread of blue *smoke* from a wood fire came up from the top of the tree, and Nutkin peeped through the key-hole and sang—

"A house full, a hole full!
And you cannot gather a bowl-full!"

THE TALE OF SQUIRREL NUTKIN

The squirrels searched for nuts all over the island and filled their little sacks.

But Nutkin gathered oak-apples— yellow and scarlet—

THE TALE OF SQUIRREL NUTKIN

and sat upon a beech-stump playing marbles, and watching the door of old Mr. Brown.

THE TALE OF SQUIRREL NUTKIN

On the third day the squirrels got up very early and went fishing; they caught seven fat minnows as a present for Old Brown.

They paddled over the lake and landed under a crooked chest-nut tree on Owl Island.

THE TALE OF SQUIRREL NUTKIN

THE TALE OF SQUIRREL NUTKIN

Twinkleberry and six other little squirrels each carried a fat minnow; but Nutkin, who had no nice manners, brought no present at all.

THE TALE OF SQUIRREL NUTKIN

He ran in front, singing—

"The man in the wilderness said to me,
  'How many strawberries grow in the sea?'
  I answered him as I thought good—
  'As many red herrings as grow in the wood.'"

But old Mr. Brown took no interest in riddles—not even when the answer was provided for him.

On the fourth day the squirrels brought a present of six fat beetles, which were as good as plums in *plum-pudding* for Old Brown. Each beetle was wrapped up carefully in a dock-leaf, fastened with a pine-needle pin.

THE TALE OF SQUIRREL NUTKIN

But Nutkin sang as rudely as ever—

"Old Mr. B! riddle-me-ree
Flour of England, fruit of Spain,
Met together in a shower of rain;
Put in a bag tied round with a string,
If you'll tell me this riddle, I'll give you a ring!"

Which was ridiculous of Nutkin, because he had not got any ring to give to Old Brown.

THE TALE OF SQUIRREL NUTKIN

THE TALE OF SQUIRREL NUTKIN

The other squirrels hunted up and down the nut bushes; but Nutkin gathered robin's pin-cushions off a briar bush, and stuck them full of pine-needle pins.

THE TALE OF SQUIRREL NUTKIN

On the fifth day the squirrels brought a present of wild honey; it was so sweet and sticky that they licked their fingers as they put it down upon the stone. They had stolen it out of a bumble *bees'* nest on the tippitty top of the hill.

But Nutkin skipped up and down, singing—

THE TALE OF SQUIRREL NUTKIN

THE TALE OF SQUIRREL NUTKIN

"Hum-a-bum! buzz! buzz! Hum-a-bum buzz!
  As I went over Tipple-tine
  I met a flock of bonny swine;
Some yellow-nacked, some yellow backed!
  They were the very bonniest swine
  That e'er went over Tipple-tine."

THE TALE OF SQUIRREL NUTKIN

Old Mr. Brown turned up his eyes in disgust at the impertinence of Nutkin.
But he ate up the honey!

THE TALE OF SQUIRREL NUTKIN

The squirrels filled their little sacks with nuts.

But Nutkin sat upon a big flat rock, and played ninepins with a crab apple and green fir-cones.

THE TALE OF SQUIRREL NUTKIN

THE TALE OF SQUIRREL NUTKIN

On the sixth day, which was Saturday, the squirrels came again for the last time; they brought a new-laid *egg* in a little rush basket as a last parting present for Old Brown.

But Nutkin ran in front laughing, and shouting—

THE TALE OF SQUIRREL NUTKIN

"Humpty Dumpty lies in the beck,
  With a white counterpane round his neck,
  Forty doctors and forty wrights,
  Cannot put Humpty Dumpty to rights!"

THE TALE OF SQUIRREL NUTKIN

THE TALE OF SQUIRREL NUTKIN

THE TALE OF SQUIRREL NUTKIN

Now old Mr. Brown took an interest in eggs; he opened one eye and shut it again. But still he did not speak.

THE TALE OF SQUIRREL NUTKIN

Nutkin became more and more
impertinent—

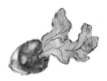

THE TALE OF SQUIRREL NUTKIN

THE TALE OF SQUIRREL NUTKIN

"Old Mr. B! Old Mr. B!
Hickamore, Hackamore, on the King's kitchen door;
All the King's horses, and all the King's men,
Couldn't drive Hickamore, Hackamore,
Off the King's kitchen door."

Nutkin danced up and down like a *sunbeam;* but still Old Brown said nothing at all.

THE TALE OF SQUIRREL NUTKIN

Nutkin began again—

> "Arthur O'Bower has broken his band,
> He comes roaring up the land!
> The King of Scots with all his power,
> Cannot turn Arthur of the Bower!"

Nutkin made a whirring noise to sound like the *wind,* and he took a running jump right onto the head of Old Brown! . . .

THE TALE OF SQUIRREL NUTKIN

THE TALE OF SQUIRREL NUTKIN

Then all at once there was a flutter-
ment and a scufflement and a loud
"Squeak!"

The other squirrels scuttered away into
the bushes.

THE TALE OF SQUIRREL NUTKIN

When they came back very cautiously, peeping round the tree—there was Old Brown sitting on his door-step, quite still, with his eyes closed, as if nothing had happened.

THE TALE OF SQUIRREL NUTKIN

56

THE TALE OF SQUIRREL NUTKIN

*　　*　　*　　*　　*

But Nutkin was in his waist-coat pocket!
This looks like the end of the story;
but it isn't.

THE TALE OF SQUIRREL NUTKIN

Old Brown carried Nutkin into his house, and held him up by the tail, intending to skin him; but Nutkin pulled so very hard that his tail broke in two,

THE TALE OF SQUIRREL NUTKIN

and he dashed
up the staircase
and escaped out
of the attic window.

THE TALE OF SQUIRREL NUTKIN

And to this day, if you meet Nutkin up a tree and ask him a riddle, he will throw sticks at you, and stamp his feet and scold, and shout—

"Cuck-cuck-cuck-cur-r-r-cuck-k-k!"

THE TALE OF SQUIRREL NUTKIN

Don't miss these other Beatrix Potter favorites from Bantam Books:
THE TALE OF PETER RABBIT
THE TALE OF BENJAMIN BUNNY
THE TALE OF MRS. TIGGY-WINKLE
THE TALE OF MR. JEREMY FISHER
THE TAILOR OF GLOUCESTER
CECILY PARSLEY'S NURSERY RHYMES
THE TALE OF TOM KITTEN
THE TALE OF TWO BAD MICE
THE TALE OF JEMIMA PUDDLE-DUCK
THE ROLY-POLY PUDDING

ISBN 0-553-15205-X